Dear Parent:
Your child's love of reading starts here!

Every child learns to read in a different way and at his or her own speed. Some go back and forth between reading levels and read favorite books again and again. Others read through each level in order. You can help your young reader improve and become more confident by encouraging his or her own interests and abilities. From books your child reads with you to the first books he or she reads alone, there are I Can Read Books for every stage of reading:

SHARED READING
Basic language, word repetition, and whimsical illustrations, ideal for sharing with your emergent reader

BEGINNING READING
Short sentences, familiar words, and simple concepts for children eager to read on their own

READING WITH HELP
Engaging stories, longer sentences, and language play for developing readers

READING ALONE
Complex plots, challenging vocabulary, and high-interest topics for the independent reader

ADVANCED READING
Short paragraphs, chapters, and exciting themes for the perfect bridge to chapter books

I Can Read Books have introduced children to the joy of reading since 1957. Featuring award-winning authors and illustrators and a fabulous cast of beloved characters, I Can Read Books set the standard for beginning readers.

A lifetime of discovery begins with the magical words **"I Can Read!"**

Visit www.icanread.com for information
on enriching your child's reading experience.

*To Craig George, who was
imprinted as "mother" on the wild
pets Goose and Duck.
That's how it is with birds.*
—J.C.G.

To David, for all his love and support
—P.L.

HarperCollins®, ✎®, and I Can Read Book® are trademarks of HarperCollins Publishers Inc.

Goose and Duck   Text copyright © 2008 by Julie Productions Inc.   Illustrations copyright © 2008 by Priscilla Lamont
Library of Congress Cataloging-in-Publication Data
George, Jean Craighead, date.
   Goose and Duck / by Jean Craighead George ; illustrated by Priscilla Lamont.— 1st ed.
      p.   cm.
   Summary: A young boy becomes the "mother" to a goose, who becomes "mother" to a duck, as they learn about the rhythms of
nature together
      ISBN-10: 0-06-117076-3 (trade bdg.) — ISBN-13: 978-0-06-117076-8 (trade bdg.)
      ISBN-10: 0-06-117077-1 (lib. bdg.) — ISBN-13: 978-0-06-117077-5 (lib. bdg.)
      [1. Human-animal relationships—Fiction.   2. Geese—Fiction.   3. Ducks—Fiction.]   I. Lamont, Priscilla, ill.   II. Title.
PZ7.G2933Goo 2008   2006021715
[E]—dc22   CIP
                                                                                                                AC

Typography by Jaime Morrell   13 14 15 SCP 10 9 8 7   ❖   First Edition

I Can Read!™

READING
2
WITH HELP

Goose and Duck

by Jean Craighead George

Illustrated by Priscilla Lamont

LAURA GERINGER BOOKS

An Imprint of HarperCollinsPublishers

I found an egg by the lake.

It cracked open in the grass.

A little goose wiggled
out of the shell.

He stared at me.

I stared at him.

And I became his mother.

That's how it is with birds.

I took him home and fed him.

Whatever I did, Goose did.

When I sat down, Goose sat down.

When I ate at the table,

Goose ate at the table.

When I hopped, Goose hopped.

When I went to bed,

Goose went to bed.

Then I found a duck egg.

A duckling hatched and saw Goose.

Goose stared at the duckling.

And Goose became his mother.

Whatever I did, Goose did.

Whatever Goose did, Duck did.

When I sat down, Goose sat down.

Duck sat down too.

When I ate at the table,

Goose ate at the table.

And Duck ate at the table too.

When I stood on my hands,

Goose went upside down.

And Duck went upside down too.

When I went to bed,

Goose went to bed.

And Duck went to bed too.

One night there was a full moon.

Duck and Goose woke up.

"Quack!"

Duck called for his mother.

"Honk!"

Goose called for his mother.

But I was asleep in my bed.

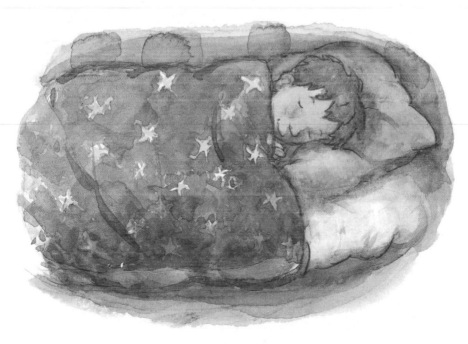

Goose and Duck called louder.

They walked onto the sidewalk.

"Honk!" said Goose.

"Quack! Quack!" said Duck.

A policeman drove down our street.

He heard the noise.

The moon went behind a cloud.

It was very dark.

Goose thought the policeman was me.

Goose flew into the police car
and sat beside his mother.
Duck flew into the police car
and sat beside his mother.

The policeman closed the door
and drove to the police station.

The next morning my neighbor said,

"Goose and Duck were arrested!"

I got on my bike

and rode to the police station.

The policeman was washing his car.

Goose was flapping his wings.

He was having a good time in the water.

Duck was flapping his wings
and having a good time too.

"Hello," I said to the policeman.

"I have come

to get my goose and duck."

"Your goose and duck?"

said the policeman.

"They sit down when I sit down,"
I said.

"They sit down when I sit down too,"
said the policeman.

I went into the police station
to see the captain.

Goose went into the police station.

Duck went into the police station too.

"Hello," I said to the captain.

"May I have

my goose and duck back?"

Goose flew to the captain's desk.

Duck flew to the captain's desk too.

Papers swirled and spun in the air.

"You can have them!"

shouted the Captain.

"Just take them away!"

I walked out of the police station.

Goose walked out of the police station.

Duck walked out of the police station.

"Good-bye," the policeman said,

waving to Goose and Duck.

When the leaves fell from the trees,
Goose stared up into the sky.
Geese were honking and flying south
for the winter.

Suddenly Goose knew who he was.

He flapped his wings

and joined the geese.

The next day

Duck stared up into the sky.

Ducks were quacking

and flying south.

Suddenly Duck knew who he was too.

He flapped his wings
and joined the ducks.

And I know who I am.

I am a boy

who was mother to a goose

who was mother to a duck.

Then Goose and Duck grew up
and flew away.

That's how it is with birds.